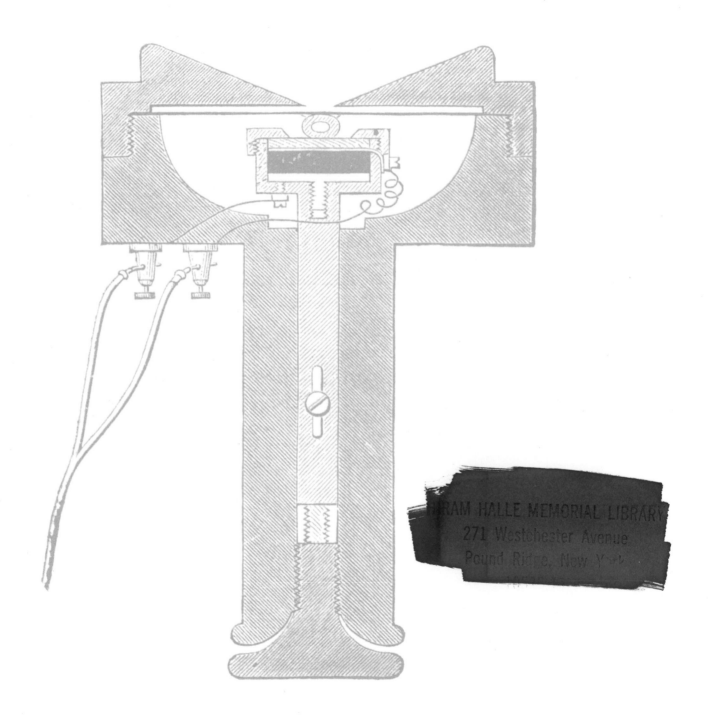

THE TELEPHONE

TURNING POINT INVENTIONS

THE TELEPHONE

SARAH GEARHART
Foldout illustration by Toby Welles

Atheneum Books for Young Readers

Atheneum Books for Young Readers
An imprint of Simon & Schuster
Children's Publishing Division
1230 Avenue of the Americas
New York, New York 10020

FIRST EDITION

Produced by
CommonPlace Publishing
2 Morse Court
New Canaan, Connecticut 06840

Art Director: Samuel N. Antupit
Editor: Sharon AvRutick
Picture Research: Jean Martin
Production Design: Cheung/Crowell Design

Printed in Hong Kong through Global Interprint

10 9 8 7 6 5 4 3 2 1

ISBN 0-689-82815-2

Library of Congress
Card Catalog Number: 98-89823

For Jerry and for Gemma

Page 1
This photograph of the telephone's inventor, Alexander Graham Bell, was taken in 1873.
Pages 2–3
The Princess Telephone, introduced in 1959, offered a popular new look including a choice of designer colors and an illuminated dial.

Picture Credits

Sally Andersen-Bruce: pages 2–3.

Antique Wireless Association: pages 1, 8, 29(top), 31(both), 32, 41(top left and right), 44(top, bottom left), 45, 47, 58, 61(center).

Archive Photos: pages 6, 13, 15, 77.

AT&T Archives: page 75(right).

The Boy Scout Handbook (1911): page 10.

Canadian Heritage, Parks Canada AGBNHS: page 19.

Courtesy George Eastman House: page 63.

The Grosvenor Collection: pages 24(both), 26, 59.

Hollywood Book & Poster: page 69 (bottom left).

Library of Congress: pages 16, 21, 25, 29(bottom), 42, 72.

© Estate of Roy Lichtenstein: *Oh Jeff... I Love You Too, But,* 1964, Acrylic on canvas, 48"x48", Private Collection: page 69(bottom right).

Lucent Technologies Bell Labs Innovations: pages 41(top center, bottom), 44(bottom right), 66–67(top 10, bottom 6).

Collection of Rick Marschall: page 76.

Motorola: page 74(right).

The New York Public Library Picture Collection: pages 11, 14, 46, 69(top right).

NYNEX Pioneers: pages 60, 65, 74(left), 75(left).

The Pac Bell Archives and Museum: pages 57, 61, 62, 64, 69(top left).

Smithsonian Institution: page 30(both).

Ted Spiegel: pages 70–71.

Superstock: pages 9, 35.

Telephone History Group/US West: pages 36–37, 37, 67(far right bottom).

Original artwork by Toby Welles: pages 49–54.

CONTENTS

1

BEFORE THE TELEPHONE

Who did you talk to today? Was it face to face or by telephone? Did you send or receive any faxes or E-mail? Did you use the Internet to do your homework?

Without the telephone, there would be no Internet, E-mail, or faxes. If you weren't able to visit friends in person, you'd have to write letters and depend on the mail system to deliver them. It would take longer — much longer — to give and receive much of the information that we rely on having every day.

For most of human history, long-distance communication — especially if you wanted to communicate quickly — was very difficult or even impossible. Hundreds and hundreds of years ago, one of the fastest ways to get an urgent message to someone who was farther away than shouting distance was to build a fire or light a torch on a hilltop or tower. Of course, your message would have to be pretty simple. For example, one fire or torch might mean "The enemy is coming." Two might mean "The coast is clear."

Native Americans actually developed a more complex system of signaling with fire by controlling the release of the smoke, but such smoke signals certainly had their limitations — the need for clear weather and little or no wind were only two of them.

Opposite
For centuries before the telegraph and the telephone, writing a letter was the fastest way to communicate over a long distance. At first, only the most highly educated and highly placed members of a community, like this "writing master," wrote at all, and writing itself was a complicated and time-consuming art. There was no store-bought paper or ink, and writing instruments were all made by hand. Letters were delivered by a person on foot or by horseback and, depending on their destination, took days or months to arrive.

Another way to send a message between places that weren't too far apart was to use sounds that carried better than the human voice. Some African tribes, for example, traditionally have communicated with their neighbors using drums. Drummers of such "talking drums" use a variety of rhythms to express a wide range of ideas.

Thousands of years ago, if you needed to get a message to a friend beyond the range of sight or sound, however, the only way to do it was by word of mouth. The time it took for the message to be delivered depended on the mode of transportation at hand. At first, the only way a messenger would be able to get around would have been on foot. In Asia, archaeologists have found evidence of Stone Age couriers who would run from place to place carrying messages as long ago as the fifteenth century B.C.

When writing was developed, around 3500 B.C., messengers no longer had to rely on their memories, and the messages themselves could be longer

8

The American painter John Mix Stanley (1814–1872) portrayed the Native American practice of sending smoke signals to convey messages in his painting *Indian Telegraph*.

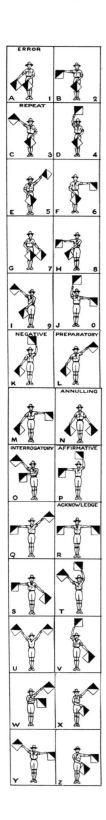

and more complicated. And when people learned to use horses for transportation (by at least the fifth century B.C.), messengers could go much faster. One nineteenth-century message-delivery system that relied on horses, the Pony Express, became famous. It was a system of riders carrying mail in relays a distance of nearly two thousand miles between St. Joseph, Missouri, and Sacramento, California. The average trip took about ten days. While it made delivery time much shorter, the Pony Express has lived on much longer in memory than it did in real life, for the remarkable technological changes of the nineteenth century made it unnecessary soon after it was set up.

As the nineteenth century dawned, though, things were not much different than they'd been for literally thousands of years before. The few roads that existed in the United States didn't go very far and were usually unpaved and poorly maintained. Most people still grew up without traveling or even sending messages much farther than fifty miles from where they lived. Steam speeded things up, but — as Americans would soon see — it was nothing compared to the power of electricity.

By the early 1800s, several men — most of them scientists in Europe — had made discoveries about electricity's ability to travel almost instantly along a wire from one point to another, no matter the distance between the points. Some had also experimented with using electricity to send signals that represented messages. But it was Samuel F. B. Morse, a young American painter with no formal training in science, who finally designed a machine and a code of signals that turned electricity's potential for communication into a reality. Returning home from Paris in 1832, Morse sketched a rough plan for what became the first practical electromagnetic telegraph in America.

Congress passed a bill allowing the construction of an experimental telegraph line in February 1843. Morse chose Washington, D.C., to Baltimore as the route and got permission to run the line alongside the tracks of the Baltimore & Ohio Railroad, although the railroad insisted on the right to remove it if it interfered with the trains. Construction began in Washington that

fall. At first, the workers dug trenches and buried the wires in pipes underground, but they soon discovered that stringing the wires on evenly spaced poles aboveground was more effective.

On May 1, 1844 — when they were still fifteen miles from their final destination — Morse and his team had an opportunity to see the success of the new system. Henry Clay was nominated for the presidency that day at the Whig Party convention in Baltimore. The news was delivered by train to the beginning of the telegraph line and then telegraphed from there to Washington. The train reached the capital city an hour and a half after the telegram had arrived.

When the forty-mile line had been completed, on May 24, Morse sent the first official message from the Supreme Court to the new telegraph office in the railroad station in downtown Baltimore: "What hath God wrought!"

Those words from the Bible would seem almost an understatement by 1866 when telegraph lines reached as far west as California and under the Atlantic as far east as England, with over 100,000 miles of wire connecting the cities and towns of the United States in between. But for the first few years after the opening of the Washington-Baltimore line, growth was very slow and popular enthusiasm even slower. Fortunately, Morse found a man who could see the potential of the telegraph, especially for American business, and could sell the idea to the people who would pay.

Amos Kendall had been the United States postmaster general for five years before the introduction of the telegraph, and he knew all the commercial routes in the country. He quickly saw the advantage of having telegraph lines run along those routes. Although he and Morse's other partners had to put up money themselves for the next lines — from New York City to Washington and Boston — once those were in operation, the advantage became clear to outside investors as well. By the 1850s, there were dozens of fledgling telegraph companies in operation.

Besides businesspeople who could now telegraph orders back and forth and trace shipments more easily, journalists were among the first to send and receive messages along the new wires. Before the telegraph, newspapers had been local in the truest sense. News from other parts of the country or from overseas was stale by the time it arrived in the regular mail. As telegraph lines spread, it became possible to get reports of events in far-off places on the very day they happened. At first newspapers in the same area competed fiercely with each other to get the stories first from telegraph offices. Eventually they began to band together, and eventually they started their own shared telegraph services to collect the main domestic and foreign news.

Ultimately, the train and the telegraph not only helped each other, but along with better roads, inland waterways, and steam-powered boats, eventually formed a complex system of transportation and communication linking city to country, north to south, coast to coast, even continent to continent, with a speed undreamed of in the "old days" of dirt roads and rivers, horses and sailboats.

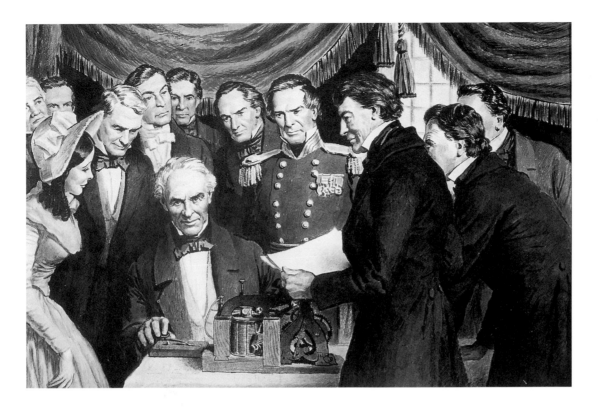

The telegraph was perhaps the most powerful partner in this new network, coordinating the movement of people, products, and information across America and Europe, seeming to overcome the barriers of time and space. As a poet of the time put it, "'We are one,' said the nations, and hand met hand / In a thrill electric from land to land."

But despite its speed and reach, even the telegraph had its limits. It required a skilled operator who knew Morse code and was able to work the instrument. And the speed of the message depended on how quickly and accurately the operator hit the key. (The fastest averaged about forty words per minute.)

If you wanted to send a telegram, you'd start by writing out your message. Then you'd have to bring it to a telegraph office where a special operator would translate each word into a code of short signals (dots) and long ones (dashes) that could be sent over a wire to the telegraph office closest to the per-

Opposite
Samuel F. B. Morse (1791–1872), an American painter and inventor of the telegraph, devised the Morse code, a system of dots and dashes that represent numbers and letters.

Above
On May 24, 1844, Morse sent the first official message by telegraph from the Supreme Court Chamber in the Capitol Building in Washington, D.C., to the railway station in downtown Baltimore, forty miles away. The words were from the Bible: "What hath God wrought!"

son you were sending it to. At the other end, the dots and dashes would be translated back into your words and — finally — delivered.

Another problem with sending telegrams was the cost. You would be charged according to the length of the message and the distance it had to go. To send a message the 448 miles from Boston to Washington, D.C., in 1876, for instance, cost 75 cents for the first ten words, more than half a day's pay for the average working person of the time.

While many people couldn't afford to send even one message, the richest in the big cities were soon able to install telegraph call boxes at home. By turning a crank on the box a certain number of times, a signal would be sent for a doctor, or firefighters, or a police officer to come — for example, five turns might summon a doctor, six the fire department, and so on — or for a

messenger to take the words of the message to the nearest telegraph office.

In early 1876, few people living in Boston — or anywhere else, for that matter — could have dreamed of any means of communication better than the telegraph. In fact, many people felt that the telegraph was a brilliant device that would never be improved upon. "It is the first human invention which is obviously final," wrote one historian. "Here, for the first time, the human mind has reached the utmost limit of its progress."

And yet, right there in Boston, in a makeshift laboratory on Exeter Place, a twenty-nine-year-old teacher was at work inventing an instrument that would allow nearly everyone, no matter where they lived, to communicate directly with each other — and not in a code but in their own voices. Alexander Graham Bell was on the verge of making the first working model of the telephone.

Although the telephone took over some of the business of the telegraph, the two continued to operate side by side well into the twentieth century. Telegrams were still used to deliver messages on special occasions — and sometimes the messengers delivered the message in song.

15

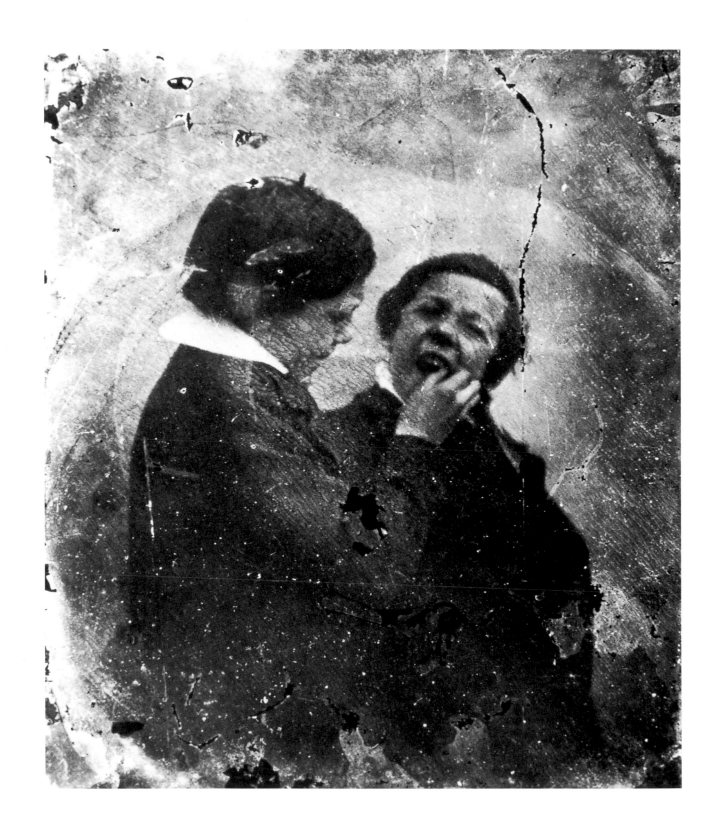

2

THE INVENTOR'S LIFE

The inventor of the telephone was born in Edinburgh, Scotland, on March 3, 1847. The two Alexanders before him, his father and his grandfather, were both elocutionists, teachers of the art of correct speech. By the time of the third Alexander's birth, his father, known by his middle name, Melville, was already a successful lecturer and public reader of such popular authors as Charles Dickens. His mother, Eliza, was a portrait painter and a talented pianist, even though she could hear only by means of a trumpet-shaped "ear tube" that made sounds louder.

Aleck, as his family called him, would bring together the influences of both his parents in his own life. Like his father, he studied the way human beings speak. He then applied his knowledge to helping those who, like his mother, had trouble speaking because they couldn't hear. His interests in understanding and improving our ability to communicate with each other eventually led him to his great invention.

But it took a while for his interests to emerge. Until he was ten, his mother taught him at home, and he didn't appear to be especially gifted at anything — except the piano. He was able to play almost any tune he heard as long as he was playing by ear. To encourage his talent, his mother arranged for him to

Opposite
Alexander Graham Bell's father, Alexander Melville Bell, was an early enthusiast of the new art of photography. He had a darkroom and taught his sons to process and develop shots like this one, which shows Aleck examining his brother Ted's mouth — early evidence of his interest in the anatomy of speech.

Such demonstrations added to Aleck's growing knowledge of the mechanics of speech and got him interested in doing some research of his own. Back at Weston House, he started studying the formation and sounds of vowels. First he noted the positions of the mouth and tongue associated with each vowel. Then he vibrated tuning forks of various pitches until he created a sound that matched the sound of the vowel. He realized that each vowel actually consisted of more than one pitch.

In 1866 his father suggested that Aleck send the results of his experiments to Alexander J. Ellis, an expert on sound. Ellis wrote back to congratulate Aleck but pointed out that the discovery had already been made by a German scientist named Hermann von Helmholtz, who had reproduced the "compound pitch" of vowels with a number of tuning forks vibrated by electromagnets — pieces of iron wrapped with wire and magnetized by a battery-powered current flowing through the wire.

Although he may have been disappointed to find out that his work wasn't original, Aleck must have been pleased to know that by himself he had arrived at the same conclusion as a famous scientist. From Ellis, Aleck may also have gotten the impression that Helmholtz had used electricity to send vowel sounds with tuning forks. If so, it was a false impression, though it did encourage the young man to learn something about electricity.

Grandfather Bell had died in 1865, leaving his house in London to Aleck's parents. To be closer to his family, Aleck took a new teaching job in Bath, England, in the fall of 1866. There, after school, he taught himself about batteries and made a telegraph with a needle like Wheatstone's, with which he communicated with a neighbor.

He spent only one year in Bath. In the spring of 1867, his brother Ted, who had been sick for months, died of tuberculosis, a disease for which there was no treatment in the nineteenth century. That summer Aleck moved to London to be with his grieving parents.

Over the next three years, he continued reading and experimenting, took courses in anatomy and medicine at University College London, and helped his father promote *Visible Speech*, which was finally published in 1867. He may also have conceived the idea that was to fuel his experiments for nearly ten more years. His work with tuning forks and his understanding (or misunderstanding) of what Helmholtz had done seems to have combined with his later study of electricity and the telegraph to suggest to him that it would be possible to send several messages at once over a single telegraph wire, as long as each message was of a different pitch and there were receivers at the other end tuned to separate one message — or pitch — from another. The search for the multiple telegraph was on — and a number of inventors were furiously working on the problem.

Visible Speech led to another idea, one to which Aleck would be devoted for the rest of his life: His father thought that the principles of the system could be used to show the deaf how to make the sounds they couldn't hear. In the spring of 1868, Aleck started testing it on deaf children at a private school in London, with enough success that his father began to recommend the practice in his lectures about the book.

Still, it was a sad and discouraging time for the family. The book wasn't bringing Melville Bell the attention — or the income — he'd hoped for. Their youngest son was gone, and by 1870 Melville and Eliza learned that Melly, too, had tuberculosis. Aleck's own health was shaky. He suffered from bad headaches and had trouble sleeping. When Melly died in May, a new beginning in a new land may have seemed the best hope for the survivors. Melville had been on a book tour in America the year before and on his way home stopped to see friends in Canada, where he had visited as a young man. He decided to resettle there with his remaining family.

Aleck was understandably reluctant to go. He had begun to establish himself in London, where he had the advantage of his grandfather's connections and a growing acquaintance with men like Wheatstone and Ellis who could help him with his work. He had access to a fine university as well as everything

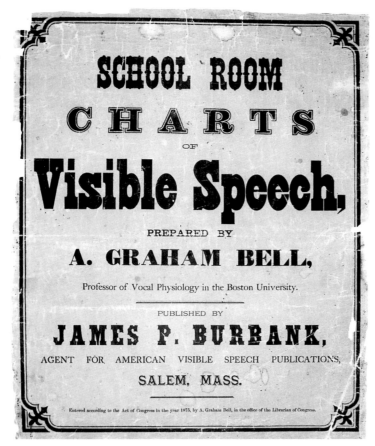

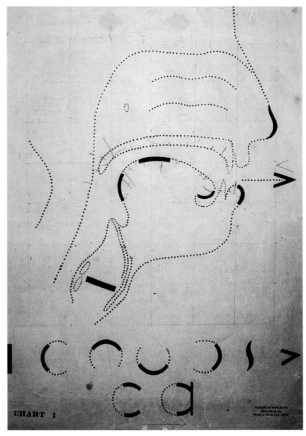

CHART I

Bell developed charts based on his father's system of Visible Speech to help his deaf students see how sounds were formed. The diagrams showed the positions of the mouth, lips, and tongue, which were indicated by the symbols on the bottom of the picture.

else the city had to offer. He didn't want to give it all up for the "backwoods of Canada," as he told his mother. But he was now his parents' only child and he couldn't let them go without him.

When Aleck boarded the ship for Canada, he had with him a copy of Helmholtz's book, *On the Sensations of Tone,* as well as a new diary, which he had entitled "Thought Book of A. Graham Bell." Even though the thought of it hadn't yet occurred to him, he also took along much of the background in sound and electricity he'd draw on to invent the telephone. Thus equipped, on July 21, 1870, Alexander Graham Bell headed not only for the New World, which would be his home for the rest of his life, but for the new world he would create with his invention.

Aleck helped his father classify the different vowels for Visible Speech by studying how they were produced. Using tuning forks, he found that each vowel sound was actually made up of a combination of pitches. His work impressed Alexander J. Ellis, a prominent expert on speech of the time, and led to further experiments that eventually culminated in the invention of the telephone.

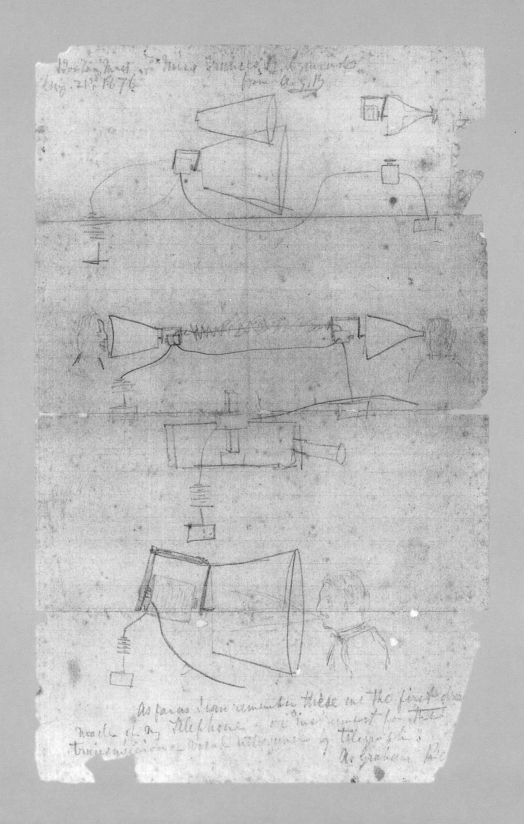

3
INVENTING THE TELEPHONE

The Bells landed in Quebec on August 1, 1870, and went directly to stay with their friends the Hendersons in a town called Paris in the province of Ontario. Within a week they had bought a house and ten acres of property near the neighboring town of Brantford, about forty-five miles west of Buffalo, New York. Soon after they moved in, Melville Bell set off on another book and lecture tour through Canada and the United States.

Aleck spent the next few months resting and trying to get rid of his headaches. He found that the "backwoods" agreed with him, just as they had with his father so many years before. At the edge of the family's new property was a bluff overlooking the Grand River. There Aleck found a spot he called his "dreaming place," where he would take a blanket and his books and just lie for hours, reading and thinking.

Meanwhile, Melville Bell was dreaming up other plans for his son. Everywhere he went, people asked him about using Visible Speech to help the deaf speak. A woman named Sarah Fuller who had started a public school for deaf children in Boston offered him a teaching job there. Having worked so long to develop the system, Melville Bell didn't want to teach it. But he thought his son Aleck might.

Opposite
According to Bell's note at the bottom of this sketch, "As far as I can remember these are the first drawings made of my telephone — or the instrument for the transmission of vocal utterances by telegraph." The middle drawing, showing one person speaking into a transmitter and another with an ear to the receiver, is a rough version of one of the diagrams that Bell submitted with his first patent application for "Improvements in Telegraphy."

Fully recovered, Aleck took the job, starting in the spring term of 1871. He was an immediate success. In two days he had the deaf children saying words for the first time. News of his accomplishments traveled quickly, and soon a school in Northampton, Massachusetts, and another in Hartford, Connecticut, offered him jobs as well.

When the Visible Speech symbols showing the position of the mouth and tongue for each sound were not enough to demonstrate how a student should make a certain sound, Aleck would have his students touch his throat while he pronounced the sound in question so they could feel the difference.

"Does the voice in your throat *shake* while talking?" a student once asked him. "The air is always shaking when I make voice," he told her. If only he could find a way to *show* the right pattern of shaking on paper — the way Visible Speech depicted the right positions — his students could practice making sounds on their own.

Boston was certainly not the "backwoods," either. It wasn't as old or as big as London, but it already had three universities and was full of writers, scholars, and scientists, many of whom had heard of Melville Bell's work and soon began to hear of Aleck's own. When he wasn't teaching, he got invitations to lecture on Visible Speech or to attend other people's lectures on the latest discoveries in the subjects that fascinated him. Even though he wasn't experimenting, he was learning more about sound and electricity. He became a full-fledged Professor of Vocal Physiology and Elocution at the newest of the three universities in the city — Boston University — in the fall of 1873.

As a professor, Bell (no longer little Aleck) now had access not only to lectures but to laboratories and equipment at the other universities. At the Massachusetts Institute of Technology that year he saw two devices that he thought could help his deaf students see sound. One was a manometric flame capsule, invented by Rudolf Koenig. When someone spoke into the mouthpiece of this device, the sound made a membrane vibrate and caused a gas-fed flame to flicker in various patterns. For Bell's purposes, the trouble with the

Opposite
A model of the phonautograph Bell constructed in 1874 using a dead man's ear. The trumpet-shaped mouthpiece funneled the sound of his speech to the eardrum, moving the small bones of the inner ear, to which one end of a piece of straw was attached. The other end of the straw traced the pattern of vibrations on a charcoal-coated glass plate moving along under the straw. The tracings recorded each sound as a continuous series of waves (*below*). Bell hoped this device would help his deaf students learn to speak by giving them the opportunity to match the tracings of their sounds to those made by people who could hear.

28

machine was that it didn't make a permanent record of its results.

But another machine did. The phonautograph, invented by Leon Scott, suggested by its name that it got the "autograph" of the sound spoken into it. It too had a membrane that vibrated in response to speech. Attached to the membrane was a reed that picked up the vibrations and drew their pattern on a piece of glass coated with charcoal. Using the phonautograph, deaf people could compare their own attempts at correct speech against this visual record of the patterns of particular sounds.

The vibrating membrane of the phonautograph reminded Bell of the human eardrum. And so, in Boston and then back in Canada during the summer of 1874, he used an actual dead man's ear to make his own version of Scott's machine. When he spoke into the eardrum, it vibrated — just like the membrane — and caused a reed attached to the bones of the inner ear to move with the vibration.

Maybe — as he later claimed — he was at his dreaming place by the river, just listening to the sounds of nature around him, when he suddenly saw a connection between his human-ear phonautograph and the multiple telegraph (by which more than one message could be sent simultaneously): If you could speak into an electrical current and get it to vibrate the way the phonautograph's reed did, you could send speech — not just coded messages or single tones — as far and as fast as electricity could travel!

This was the basic theory of the telephone, and it came to Bell when he wasn't looking for it. His conscious goals had been to show deaf children how to speak and to make a telegraph that could send many messages at once. Along the way, he had acquired knowledge about sound and electricity that

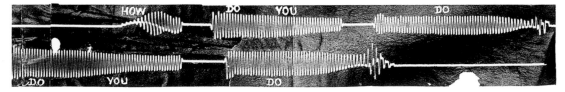

combined to put another, more far-reaching, goal in front of him.

When Bell returned to Boston in the fall, however, he decided to try to perfect the multiple telegraph before testing the new theory of the telephone — probably because the telegraph seemed an easier idea to sell. He needed money now, as soon as he could get it. His teaching salary couldn't even cover the cost of equipment for his experiments. Fortunately, two of his private pupils indirectly helped him find financing; one of them also helped him find love.

Bell commuted to his classes at Boston University from businessman Thomas Sanders' house in the suburb of Salem, where he had free room and board in exchange for tutoring Sanders' son George, who had been born deaf. After working with Bell for two years, six-year-old George could now read and was making progress learning to speak.

Bell had taken on another new pupil the year before — Mabel Hubbard, the daughter of Gardiner Greene Hubbard, a Boston lawyer who was also president of the Clarke Institution for Deaf Mutes in Northampton. Mabel had

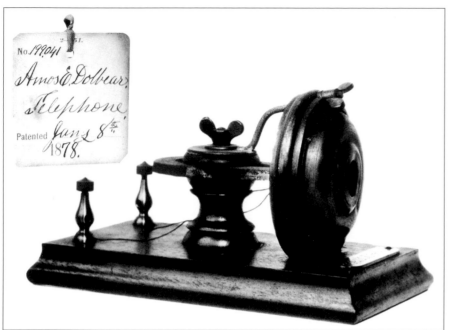

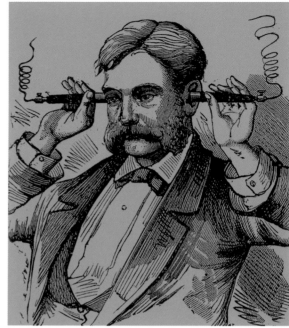

been able to hear and speak until she got scarlet fever at the age of five. Now nearly sixteen, she could still speak, but her words were hard to understand. Her father hired Bell to help her enunciate more clearly.

Mabel didn't like Professor Bell at first. He looked funny, she thought — badly dressed and "hardly a gentleman." But when he started teaching, she found him "so quick, so enthusiastic, so compelling" that she began to like him in spite of his looks. As for him, he never had a student who learned so fast.

During his sessions with Mabel, he got to know her parents. One afternoon in the fall of 1874, he stayed on for tea after a lesson and happened to tell them about his idea for the multiple telegraph, demonstrating the principle of the resonance of vowel sounds by his trick of singing into the piano and having the note echoed back.

He couldn't have chosen a better audience. Hubbard had a longtime interest in improving telegraph service in America by being able to send many messages at once over the already existing wires. He immediately offered to help

Amos E. Dolbear (*opposite, right*), a professor of physics at Tufts College, was working on an improvement of the telephone that used a metal diaphragm and permanent magnet (*above left*) at about the same time as Bell. Although Dolbear never filed for a patent himself, he later claimed that Bell had heard reports of his experiments and then stole his ideas. Another one of Dolbear's telephone designs (*above*) used a receiver mechanism that sent the signal "in one ear and out the other."

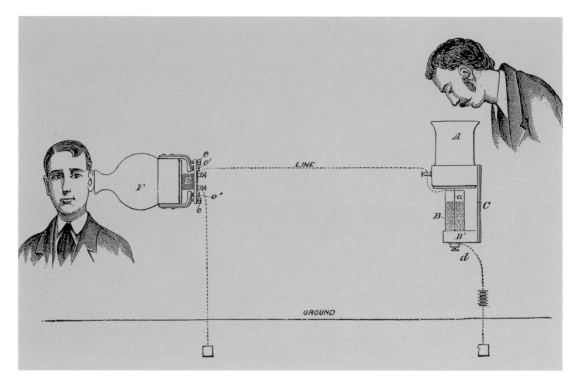

pay for Bell's experiments in return for a share of the rights to his telegraph. Thomas Sanders did the same.

Bell's own parents weren't as supportive as George's and Mabel's. His mother was afraid he would make himself sick again by working too hard. His father advised him to sell his idea to Hubbard and Sanders outright and focus on his teaching. Even Mabel — who must have been liking him more and more — became worried. "He has his machine running beautifully, but it will kill him if he is not careful," she reported to her mother.

But Bell didn't get discouraged, even though he found it hard to juggle all his responsibilities and his headaches came back.

The pressure was intense, as Hubbard urged him to work quickly. By this time, one inventor had invented a telegraph that could send two messages at a time, and Thomas Edison, who would soon invent the lightbulb, had made one that could send four. Although Hubbard believed Bell could at least double that number, he knew others — including a skilled electrician named Elisha Gray — were trying to do the same.

Bell had several problems to solve before he could complete a working model of his machine. He had already given up tuning forks for steel reeds, or strips, each with one end clamped to a metal armature and the other end able to vibrate freely over an electromagnet. By changing the length of the vibrating section of the reed, he could adjust the pitch more easily. But he still had trouble keeping each transmitter exactly tuned to its receiver. Pitches changed with the length of the wire and the strength of the battery. Sparks at the points of contact that made and broke the intermittent current sometimes caused the reeds to stop vibrating altogether. Bell needed help.

He found it at Charles Williams's Electrical Shop on Court Street in downtown Boston, where he bought most of his supplies. Thomas Watson, a young shop employee, liked solving problems for the various inventors who came in. "I made stubborn metal do my will and take the shape necessary to enable it to do its allotted work," he later wrote. With Watson's assistance, Bell was able to do his allotted work, too. By mid-February 1875, they had made a model of the multiple telegraph that Bell could take to the Patent Office in Washington.

As it turns out, Elisha Gray had gotten his application there just two days earlier. Fortunately, Bell's lawyers had advised him to make three separate patent applications, each covering different aspects of his invention. This was very important, for whoever was granted a patent on an invention would have the sole right to control it — and profit from it. Although two of Bell's applications were too much like Gray's and therefore declared to be in conflict (meaning that no patents were issued for them at this stage), Bell was granted the one he thought had the best chance for commercial use. It included his last-minute discovery of a way to record incoming messages on a strip of moving paper with a writing instrument attached to the receiver, a kind of primitive fax machine Bell called his telautograph.

While he was in Washington, Bell paid a visit to Professor Joseph Henry,

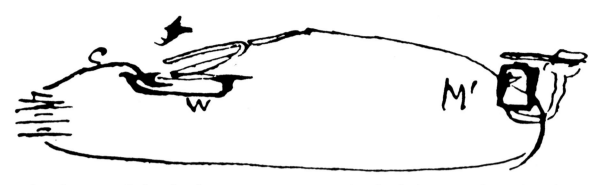

the director of the Smithsonian Institution, who had done much to lay the groundwork for the original development of the telegraph. Bell demonstrated his machine for Henry and, on the strength of Henry's approval, decided to ask the eminent scientist about his new idea for "electric speech." "Henry said he thought it was 'the germ of a great invention,'" Bell wrote his parents. And when Bell told Henry he wasn't sure he had enough understanding of electric-ity for the project, Henry simply said, "Get it!"

Back in Boston in March, happy but exhausted, Bell felt he first had to get the bugs out of his telegraph so that it could be easily manufactured and sold in large quantities under the patent he had been granted. He gave up most of his private tutoring in order to have more time to work on the telegraph, but then he didn't have enough money. He had to borrow from Watson and get an advance on his pay from the university.

One hot day in June, up in the attic rooms of the Williams's shop, he and Watson were — yet again — tuning the telegraph's transmitters and receivers. One of Watson's reeds seemed stuck. With no electrical current flowing in the circuit, he plucked it to get it going again. Suddenly Bell came running in ask-ing what he'd done. The corresponding reed in his room had made a sound! Watson plucked his reed again and the same thing happened.

What they had heard was the first recognizable sound of the telephone. The vibrations of Watson's reed close to its electromagnet had generated — or "induced" — a similarly vibrating electrical current that had activated the elec-tromagnet of Bell's receiver. The increasing and decreasing strength of mag-

Transmitters for the multiple telegraph as well as several different models of the early telephone are on display in this reconstruction of the attic workroom at Charles Williams's Electrical Shop in Boston where Bell did much of his experimenting.

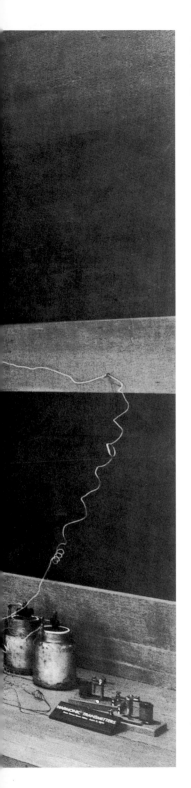

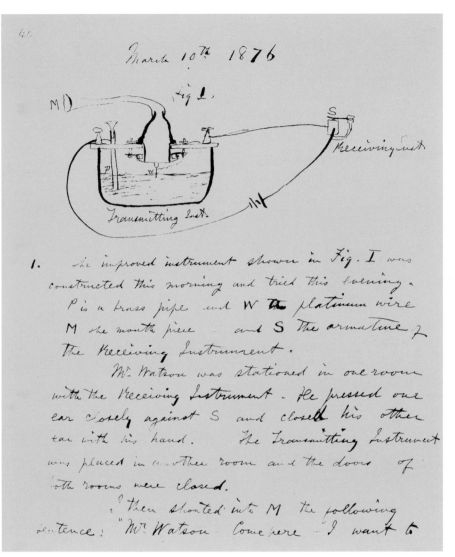

45

March 10th 1876

Fig. 1.

M)

S

Receiving Inst.

P

W

Transmitting Inst.

1. The improved instrument shown in Fig. I was constructed this morning and tried this evening. P is a brass pipe and W the platinum wire M the mouth piece — and S the armature of the Receiving Instrument.

Mr. Watson was stationed in one room with the Receiving Instrument. He pressed one ear closely against S and closed his other ear with his hand. The Transmitting Instrument was placed in another room and the doors of both rooms were closed.

I then shouted into M the following sentence: "Mr. Watson — Come here — I want to

Bell's notebook entry for March 10, 1876 — the day the telephone spoke its first words — "Mr. Watson — Come here — I want to see you." The tuning fork of March 8 had been replaced with a transmitter that had a mouthpiece (M) on one end and a membrane on the other, to which was attached a platinum wire (W) that dipped in and out of a water and acid solution when the sound of the words spoken into the mouthpiece made the membrane vibrate. The vibrations were conducted through the water to a brass pipe (P) attached to the end of the battery-powered circuit and transmitted to the receiver, causing the steel reed (S) to vibrate against Watson's ear and reproduce the sound of the words Bell had spoken into the mouthpiece.

netism caused by the increasing and decreasing vibrations of the current pulled Bell's reed in such a way that it reproduced the vibrations of Watson's reed. Just as the theory of the telephone had come to Bell when he was working on something else, so now did the earliest evidence that it might actually work. "I have accidentally made a discovery of the very greatest importance," he wrote to Hubbard that night.

Remembering the phonautograph, Bell excitedly drew up plans for a transmitter that included a membrane made from a piece of soft and pliable animal hide to use in testing the theory further. Watson made one the next day. But when they spoke into it, with a reed receiver at the other end, they could only hear faint sounds. Then the membrane broke.

Watson substituted a stronger membrane and they tried again, using a membrane receiver as well this time. The sounds were louder, but the men still couldn't make out any actual words.

It would be months before they made any more progress. Hubbard insisted they stick to the telegraph. Then Watson got sick, and by the time he was well enough to work again, Bell had other — more personal — things on his mind.

He was spending more and more time at the Hubbards, and not just because of teaching and the telegraph. He went to see Mabel, and even she was aware that their "lessons" were turning into social occasions. "I have discovered that my interest in my dear pupil has ripened into a far deeper feeling," he wrote her mother. "I have learned to love her." Since Mabel was only seventeen, her parents asked Bell to wait a year before telling her how he felt. And, though he promised he would be silent, he couldn't contain himself. Mabel wasn't thrilled, but on the other hand she didn't tell him to go away.

All this excitement interfered with Bell's work on the telegraph and telephone as well as his sleep. In September he took refuge with his family in Canada. When he returned to Boston in October, he was ready to go back to work. Even without further proof, he was so convinced that he could make a machine able to transmit speech that he began to draft a patent application.

"My present invention," he wrote, "consists in the employment of a vibratory or undulatory current of electricity in place of a merely intermittent one, and of a method for producing electrical undulation upon the line wire." By this time, he knew that there were two ways to make a current undulate, or vibrate, the way sound waves do in the air. One way was by induction: When anything (such as the vibrating reed, or the air pressure of speech itself) moves near a magnet — in its magnetic field — it produces an electric current that moves in the same way. The other way to make a current vibrate was by what's known as variable resistance — the pressure of sound waves on an already existing steady current causes the current to vibrate (or vary its resistance) in the same way as the sound. Later, Bell said that he knew "If I could make a current of electricity vary in intensity precisely as the air varies in density during the production of sound, I should be able to transmit speech telegraphically." Bell hadn't yet experimented with this principle of variable resistance — which is the principle by which the telephone still operates today — but he understood it and made a note of it in his patent application.

That year of distractions and delays took its toll on the patent application. Bell became officially engaged to Mabel at Thanksgiving, but even with that issue happily resolved, he couldn't seem to work quickly. "Procrastination is indeed my besetting sin," he confessed to his wife-to-be. When he finally finished writing the application in January 1876, he still put off filing it because he was waiting for a friend to investigate patent possibilities in England.

By now Hubbard was getting impatient. He had his own copies of the application and decided to act right away, regardless of the situation in England. Without Bell's knowledge, he had his lawyers file the application in Washington on February 14, 1876.

Once again it turned out that Bell and Elisha Gray were neck and neck. Just hours later, Gray's lawyer filed a patent caveat, or official notice, that he too was working on a "speaking telephone." "Such a coincidence has hardly happened before," Bell wrote his parents. It was a coincidence that would cause

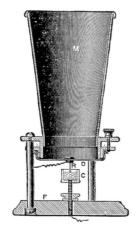

A model and diagram of one of the liquid variable-resistance transmitters Bell displayed (but did not demonstrate) at the Centennial Exhibition in Philadelphia in June 1876. Like the transmitter of the March 10 experiment, it had a membrane (D) with an attached platinum wire (R) that dipped into the liquid held in a cup (C) just below.

a lot of trouble, including many of the six hundred lawsuits in the years ahead. But because his application had been filed first, Bell would ultimately win both in the Patent Office and in court.

On his twenty-ninth birthday, March 3, 1876, he was granted U.S. Patent No. 174,465 for "Improvements in Telegraphy" — probably the best birthday gift he ever received in his life. It was the patent for the telephone, perhaps the most valuable patent ever issued and one that would make him a millionaire.

When Bell returned to his new rooms in Exeter Place in Boston, he decided to go to work right away experimenting with variable resistance, perhaps partly because the patent examiner had advised him that Gray's caveat emphasized that principle.

His first try, on March 8, was encouraging. He took a tuning fork and partially submerged its arms in a dish of water. Then he connected the tuning fork to one end of a wire and put the other end of the wire in the same dish of water, with an electromagnetic reed receiver and a battery connected in

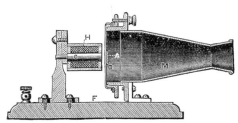

between. When he struck the arms of the tuning fork, they began to vibrate. These vibrations traveled through the water to the other end of the wire, causing the current in the circuit to vibrate. This strengthened and weakened the pull of the electromagnet, making the receiver's reed vibrate in the same way as the tuning fork, producing the tuning fork's sound in the receiver. When Bell added acid to the water, the sound got louder.

The next day, with Watson's help, he replaced the tuning fork with a membrane transmitter that had a needle attached to it. When he spoke into the membrane, it vibrated and caused the needle to dip in and out of the water, varying the current and making the receiver sound again.

On March 10, they attached a speaking tube to the transmitter box, which they set up in Bell's study. Down the hall, Watson stood in the bedroom with the receiver reed held to his ear. Suddenly he heard the words, "Mr. Watson — Come here — I want to see you." And he rushed to Bell's side to see the invention that had spoken at last.

A model and diagram of one of the electromagnetic transmitters Bell used in his demonstration of the telephone at the Centennial Exhibition. When he spoke into the mouthpiece, the metal diaphragm (D) vibrated the attached clockspring (A) in the field of the electromagnet (H), thus inducing a similarly vibrating current that was transmitted to a receiver and converted back into sound waves.

THE DAILY GRAPHIC

AN ILLUSTRATED EVENING NEWSPAPER

39 & 41 PARK PLACE

VOL. XIII. | All the News, Four Editions Daily. | NEW YORK, THURSDAY, MARCH 15, 1877. | $12 For Year in Advance. Single Copies, Five Cents. | NO. 1246.

4

A NEW WORLD

Once Hubbard had heard the telephone speak, he was anxious to let everyone else hear it too. The Centennial Exhibition that opened in Philadelphia on May 10, 1876, marking the nation's 100th anniversary, seemed like the perfect place for an American invention's first public appearance. Hubbard arranged for Bell to get a special pass to show the telephone to a panel of judges at the fair on June 25. One member of the audience was Emperor Dom Pedro of Brazil, who had met Bell at the Boston School for the Deaf and wanted to see his invention.

Bell sat the emperor at a table with his newly designed "iron box" receiver, walked to the transmitters he'd set up on the other side of the twenty-one-acre Main Building, and began reciting lines from Shakespeare into one of them. According to one account, when the amazed emperor heard the words come out of the iron box, he shouted, "My God, it talks!"

Dom Pedro's reaction was typical of those who first heard a voice over the telephone. Posters for the other demonstrations that Bell now began to give often called it the "speaking telephone" or the "talking telegraph," as though the machine itself were saying the words. People wanted to know if it could speak in numbers or foreign languages.

Opposite
A cartoonist for the New York *Daily Graphic* of March 15, 1877 captured the early fear that the telephone would be used for evil purposes, such as broadcasting the crazy ideas of lone "future orators" to captive audiences around the world, from London to San Francisco to the Fiji Islands.

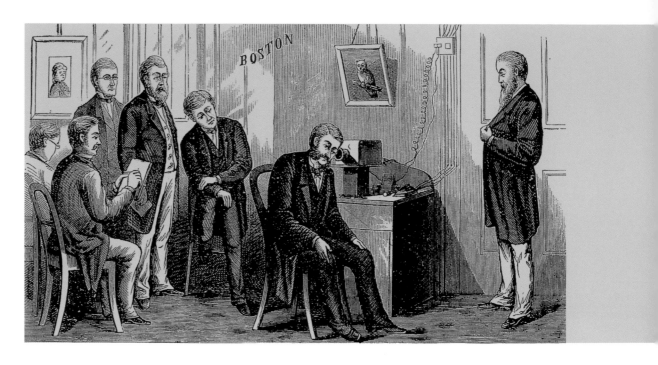

During the year after the first telephone patent had been granted, Bell and Watson gave many public demonstrations of the invention. One of the most impressive took place in Salem, Massachusetts, on February 12, 1877, using a "box" telephone, like the one *opposite bottom*. From Bell's rooms in Boston, eighteen miles away, Watson sang "Auld Lang Syne" and "Yankee Doodle" to the full house in the Lyceum Hall in Salem, which included a reporter from the *Boston Globe*. At the end of the demonstration, Bell dictated the reporter's story over the phone to a stenographer on Watson's end. It appeared the next day as "The First Newspaper Despatch Sent by a Human Voice Over the Wires."

This confusion was partly because you couldn't see the person who was talking and partly because no one had yet talked back. All the earliest calls were one-way because the first receivers could only receive, not transmit. It wasn't until October 6, 1876, that Bell and Watson had their first conversation on the telephone in the rooms at Exeter Place, using two of the membrane transmitters, which they had discovered could also act as receivers. On October 9, they talked "long distance" over a two-mile telegraph line from Boston to Cambridge. Following the success of these two experiments, Bell announced that he had arrived at the "completion of Telephony," although he did note that he realized "much doubtless yet remains to be done in perfecting the details of apparatus."

He and Watson spent the rest of the year doing just that. By using a metal sheet, or diaphragm, instead of the original membrane, and a permanent magnet — already magnetized, without the need for an electric current — instead of an electromagnet in the transmitter/receiver, they got better results.

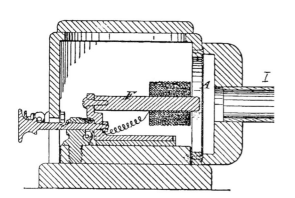

Using a permanent magnet meant that the telephone could operate without a battery. It also meant that Bell and Watson gave up the "liquid transmitter" — which, with its dish of water, wasn't really practical for commercial use — and returned to a telephone that operated by induction. In January 1877, Bell applied for and was granted a patent on the improvements. The two patents he now held — good for seventeen years each — were the basis for what

A diagram (*far left*) and a model (*left*) of the first commercial telephone (and the one used in many of Bell's public demonstrations), which served as both transmitter and receiver. The wooden box housed a metal diaphragm (A) and a permanent magnet (F). Callers spoke into the opening (I) and then put an ear against it to hear the response.

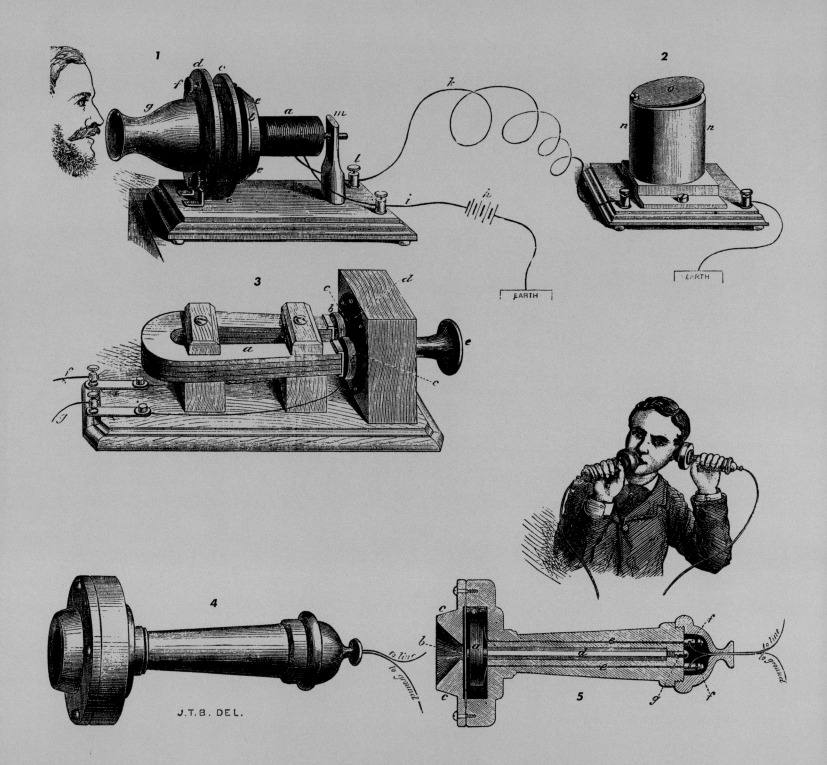

EARTH

EARTH

J.T.B. DEL.

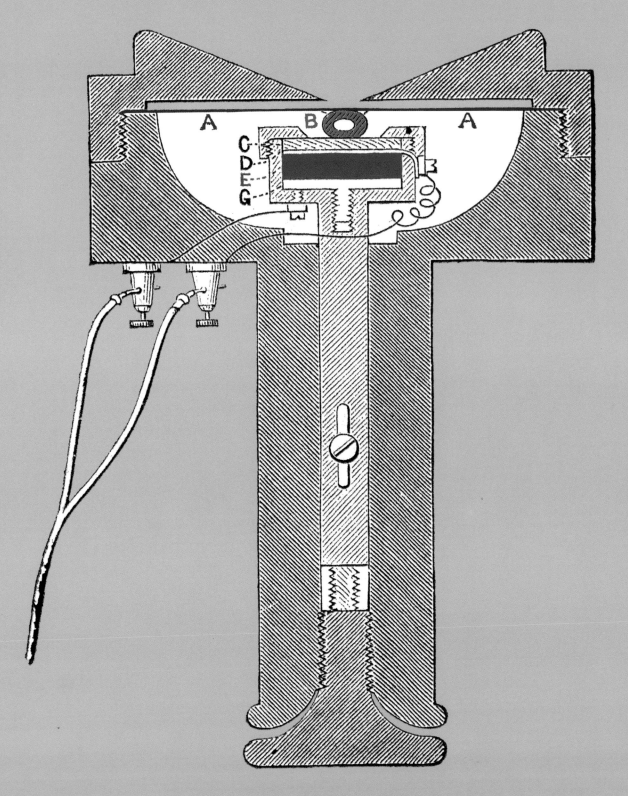

became the largest and most successful business in American history.

The first "official" telephone line ran from Charles Williams's Electrical Shop in Boston to his home in suburban Somerville. Because his shop produced all the telephone equipment, he wasn't charged for the service. The first paying customer was Roswell Downer, a friend and Somerville neighbor of Williams, who in May 1877 connected telephones to the telegraph line that already existed between his home and his downtown banking office. Nearly 200 customers had signed up before July 9, 1877, when Bell, Hubbard, Sanders, and Watson founded the Bell Telephone Company.

Having taken care of business, Bell finally felt able to assume the responsibilities of being a husband. Two days later, he and Mabel got married and set off on their honeymoon trip, leaving the telephone's immediate future in the hands of his partners.

The first advertisement from the new company listed the advantages of the telephone over the telegraph: "1st. That no skilled operator is required. . . . 2nd. That the communication is much more rapid, the average number of words transmitted a minute by Morse sounder being from fifteen to twenty, by Telephone from one to two hundred. 3rd. That no expense is required either for its operation, maintenance or repair. It needs no battery, and has no complicated machinery."

The cost for two telephones connected to each other was $20 a year for "social purposes" or $40 a year for business. All the first phones operated over telegraph lines, which the company would construct for an additional fee.

It was apparently Hubbard's idea to rent, rather than sell, the telephone equipment and to license the patent rights to agents outside of Boston. This plan not only allowed the company to keep control of the business but it also allowed the business to develop in a unified way, with standard equipment under central management.

The need for a central organization became obvious as the number of customers increased. If customers wanted to be able to make calls not just from

THE LIQUID VARIABLE-RESISTANCE TRANSMITTER

To use the liquid variable-resistance transmitter, you had to lean over and speak loudly and clearly into the vertical bell of the unit. On March 10, 1876, a device like this transmitted the first intelligible speech.

It was called the liquid transmitter because a small cup below the diaphragm contained a mixture of water and acid. A wire connected to the diaphragm was partially submerged in this fluid. At the bottom of the cup, there was one end of a battery-powered wire connected to a receiver. As the diaphragm moved up and down in response to sound in the mouthpiece, the wire went up and down with it, changing the distance that the electricity had to flow to get from the wire, through the liquid, and to the wire at the bottom of the cup. This means that a variable amount of current would flow through the liquid. These variations made up the sound signal carried on the wire to the receiver.

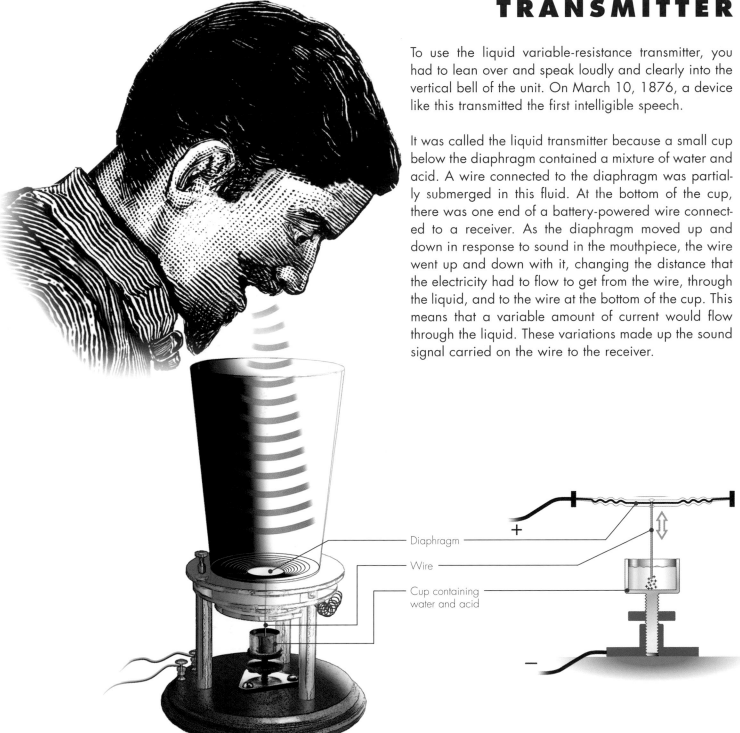

Diaphragm

Wire

Cup containing water and acid

1897 DESK SET

By the turn of the century, the telephone had graduated from being seen as a strange device to being a familiar object in the home and was styled like a piece of furniture. This design was basically unchanged for thirty years.

The earpiece was hung on the side of the phone. Low volume and poor sound quality made it difficult to hear the other party, so it was necessary to press it firmly over your ear when you used it.

The hook that held the earpiece would switch on the phone when the earpiece was lifted.

The diaphragm was housed in a large disk-shaped chamber.

The trumpet-shaped mouthpiece was shaped to amplify speech.

On early telephones there was no dial. You had to ask an operator at a switchboard in the central office to connect you manually with the line of the person you wished to talk to.

The first switchboards used metal keys (the switches) to connect each party's line to a separate "talking line" on the board. Eventually they used cords to plug each party into the talking line. This is an early-1900s "cord" switchboard at a central office. Imagine all the activity of the operators having to reach to make the right connections.

Hello Central, Give Me...

their homes to their offices, but to friends and relatives, doctors, and grocers, it would have required too many lines, and too much money, to connect each of those telephones directly to every other one. The solution was the telephone exchange, a central office where all the lines came into a switchboard.

The earliest practical switchboard connected callers manually. If you wanted to make a call, you first had to ring the central office and tell the operator the name of the person you wanted to speak to. The operator would move a metal key — the switch — attached to the end of your line to connect you to a separate "talking line" on the board, to which the line of the person you were calling would also be connected. Along with its first lines and its first customers, the telephone borrowed the idea of the exchange from the telegraph.

The first commercial telephone exchange opened in New Haven, Connecticut, in January 1878, with twenty-one subscribers. The next month it published the first telephone directory, listing the subscribers (who by then numbered fifty) by category, much like our modern Yellow Pages. Most were businesses, reflecting the pattern of telephone use that would hold true for at least the next twenty years.

One of the first New Haven subscribers, E. A. Gessner, owned a drugstore and had a phone installed so that he could take orders from the dentist across the street. A few of his braver customers would pick it up, shout into it, and then run outside to see if the dentist had heard what they said.

Using the telephone was not the automatic gesture it is today. Some people were afraid of phones and got too tongue-tied to say anything at all. Some thought they could somehow be seen over the phone and wouldn't talk on one unless they were properly dressed. Others thought it was just plain strange. The Providence *Press* reported, "It is difficult, hearing the sounds out of the mysterious box, to wholly resist the notion that the powers of darkness are somehow in league with it."

Such suspicions and fears may seem funny to us, but using the early phones — despite Bell's and Watson's improvements — was awkward enough to justify some of those feelings. The first instruments were combined transmitters and receivers. To make a call, you had to shout into — or bang on — the opening that doubled as a mouthpiece and earpiece to get the attention of the person at the other end. Then you spoke into the opening and quickly moved it to your ear to hear the response. Early instructions advised users, "Do not speak too promptly, give your correspondent time to transfer, as much trouble ensues from both parties speaking at the same time." Others warned men to "keep your mustache out of the opening."

Even if you could coordinate speaking and listening without getting your mustache caught in the equipment, it was often hard to hear what was said. Squeaks and whistles, cracking sounds and worse constantly came across the lines along with human voices. The writer Mark Twain, one of the first telephone customers but also one of its first critics, kept a daily record of the loud noises his made: "Artillery can be heard; Thunder can be heard; Artillery & thunder combined can be heard."

Certainly such technical problems help explain people's fears and show why the early phones were used most often to give business orders or take messages rather than to carry on long social conversations.

The gunfire and thunder Mark Twain heard were actually the results of the interference of natural electricity — from thunderstorms, in the atmosphere, or from stray electrical disturbances in the earth, where the ends of the lines were attached. In 1881 John J. Carty, a telephone operator who later became chief engineer of the Bell system, discovered that twisting a pair of copper wires together and using them for the circuit without attaching them to the ground cut down on strange noises. The introduction of this "local loop" made local calls quieter and calls over longer distances possible. In addition, Watson soon designed a phone with a separate transmitter and receiver, and invented first an automatic "thumper," then a buzzer, and finally a bell to signal calls. During the four years that he was master electrician for the Bell Telephone Company, he received sixty-some patents for such improvements.

Opposite
On October 18, 1892, Bell placed the first long-distance call from New York to Chicago. He spoke — surrounded by company officials, politicians, and members of the press — to William Hubbard, the nephew of Gardiner Greene Hubbard, who had assisted him in his demonstration of the telephone at the Centennial Exhibition sixteen years earlier.

Around the same time, Thomas Edison invented a way to make the voice louder and clearer, by attaching a piece of carbon to the metal diaphragm in the mouthpiece. When you spoke, the carbon transferred the vibrations of the diaphragm to the electric current in the phone.

Unfortunately for Bell and his partners, Edison sold his invention to Western Union Telegraph Company, which — despite Bell's patents — was entering the telephone business. With a well-established organization, existing telegraph lines, and a large manufacturing plant, Western Union was in a much stronger position than the fledgling Bell Telephone Company to promote and distribute the telephone. Hubbard knew that the only way they could possibly win against such odds was in court, on the grounds that Western Union was violating Bell's exclusive rights to the telephone for the term of his patents.

Bell himself was in England when the legal wheels started turning. He'd extended his honeymoon because Mabel had gotten pregnant, and they'd

stayed on for the birth of their first daughter, Elsie May. As soon as Mabel and Elsie could travel, they returned to Boston so that Bell could start preparing testimony about his invention.

The patent trial would occupy him for a full year and result in over 600 pages of evidence, including over 100 of his own. It also signaled Bell's lessening involvement with the telephone. He did participate in later lawsuits, but by this point he wanted no active part in the day-to-day business. In November 1879, to avoid a more damaging legal defeat, Western Union agreed to settle the case. In exchange for turning over all of its telephone lines and equipment and withdrawing from the market, it would receive 20 percent of the telephone rental fees from the Bell Company for the next seventeen years.

With Western Union out of the way and a new network at its disposal, the Bell Company could devote its energies to expansion. Hubbard hired Theodore Vail, who had worked for the post office as superintendent of the railway mail

Telephone poles helped eliminate some of the problems. But as the number of lines increased, and until underground cables were perfected, webs of wires crisscrossed the sky — as shown here in Pratt, Kansas, in 1909.

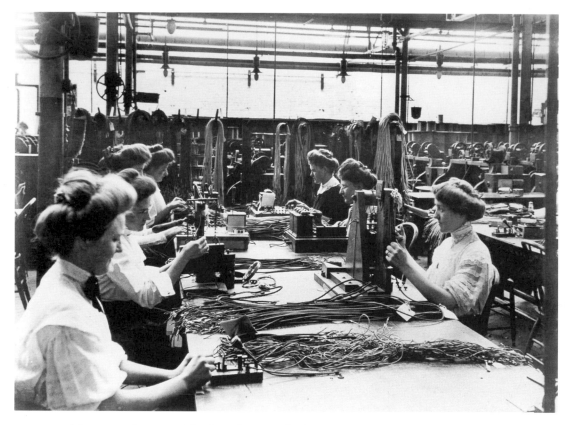

service. He was thoroughly familiar with the existing national network of transportation and communication. A lot of people thought Vail was crazy to leave a good job with a secure future for the uncertainty of a young industry. His own boss at the post office asked him to reconsider: "I can scarcely believe that a man of your sound judgment, one who holds an honorable and . . . respectable position . . . , should throw it up for a d——d old Yankee notion . . . called a telephone!" Luckily for the telephone, Vail took the job anyway and reported to the new head office in New York City in June 1878.

During the next decade, he began to construct a telephone network that would eventually exceed both the railroad and the telegraph in its ability to connect people across the country and, ultimately, around the world. By the late 1880s, Vail's network had linked the major cities in the Northeast and

Women entered the telephone industry in large numbers — and not only as operators. Here they are testing cables at the Western Electric Hawthorne Plant near Chicago around 1910.

encouraged research that would enable lines to reach even farther.

When the original patents expired in 1893 and 1894, the Bell Company faced its first real competition since Western Union. Now independent companies could manufacture their own equipment and enter the telephone business — and they did so at a rapid rate, especially in the Midwest and Far West, areas Bell had neglected as being unprofitable. In 1892 most of the 240,000 telephones in use were in the northeastern cities, in the offices of banks and other businesses or in the homes of the wealthy. By 1900, the independents had added 600,000 new customers throughout the country and, racing to stay ahead, Bell had upped its number to 800,000.

Increased competition meant lower rates, and as the telephone became affordable for the ordinary citizen, it entered — and altered — American life

Center
This sketch of an insulated copper overhead cable reveals how it is made.

Above
Better insulation meant that many telephone lines could be bundled together in an underground cable. A telephone lineman splices the wires of a cable, around 1915.

An unidentified telephone "operating room" around 1895. The female operators are seated at switchboards and supervised by the chief operator at the desk to the right.

with astonishing speed. Rural areas may have welcomed it with the most enthusiasm. Now people in small towns could pick up the phone and talk to friends in other towns, without having to take the hours a visit would entail. Farmers often got together on their own and formed telephone "co-ops" — buying their own equipment and even stringing their own lines. In some places, they didn't even bother with waiting for lines to be strung — they actually transmitted their calls over their barbed-wire fences.

The speed and convenience of telephone calls changed life in many other ways in the country and the cities. Businesses no longer had to have their offices close to their factories. People no longer had to live so close to where

they worked. Emergencies could be reported more quickly. The police could fight crime more easily. (On the other hand, criminals could also use the phone to tip each other off to the police's presence.)

As more and more people got telephones, fears about the instrument subsided and customer service improved, starting with the training of switchboard operators. The first operators were usually boys who had worked as telegraph messengers and seemed like logical — and handy — choices for the new job. But they weren't used to speaking to the public and were often rude to callers and rambunctious at work. In the 1890s, most of the boys were replaced by young women, and the operators' tones grew softer and more polite.

Correct Use of Your Phone Means <u>Good</u> Service

THE RIGHT
WAY TO TALK
KELLOGG

THE WRONG
WAY TO TALK
KELLOGG

Thurs Night
Was 16 below zero this morning. Has been below all
day. I will send you a box for Xmas tomorrow
by Express   Horace

As late as 1915, it was still necessary to show people the right way to talk on the phone, as this postcard demonstrates. You were supposed to stand close to and face the transmitter so that you could be easily heard on the other end.

Even then, there was much debate over the proper way to behave on the phone. What should you say when you answered it? Bell himself had always favored "Hoy! Hoy!" similar to the sailor's way of hailing a passing ship, as the best telephone greeting. He — and many experts on manners — thought "Hello" was too familiar and abrupt. In fact, early critics were concerned that the telephone would encourage a general decline in manners and the standards of human behavior. Mark Twain, who didn't think much of human behavior anyway, said it would have been better if Bell had invented a gag rather than a way for people to talk to each other more easily. Despite Bell and Twain and the Misses Manners of the day, "Hello" was the greeting that caught on, and the new operators were nicknamed the "Hello Girls."

The female operator quickly became an important figure in American culture. She learned to recognize the voices of all the customers on her switchboard, and they came to depend on her. A caller might say, "Central, ring me up half an hour before the 6:17 train in the morning. See if it's late, please, before you call." The operator often took messages when a call couldn't go through, listened for babies crying when their mothers had to check something on the stove, announced the time and weather, and even reported on local news. If you needed to reach the doctor, she usually knew where to find him if he wasn't in his office. She started showing up as a central character in short stories and novels and — eventually — the movies. When the automatic switchboard was introduced in 1919 and people could begin dialing their calls directly, without an operator, many felt as though they were losing a friend. Others, of course, were relieved to have privacy on the phone.

Even as customer service improved, and the phone spread into all parts of the country with the rise of the independent companies, it encountered new problems, too. Some cities now had three or four telephone companies, but customers of one couldn't call customers of any of the others. And since Bell controlled the long-distance network, if you wanted to call someone outside your city, you both had to be Bell customers.

The competition had put a serious strain on the Bell Company's finances, and even its strategy of not sharing its long-distance lines with other companies wasn't going to hold the independents off for long. In 1909, Bell's long-distance division, American Telephone and Telegraph (AT&T), merged with its old rival Western Union, and Theodore Vail became president of the largest communications company in the world. He told the stockholders in one of his first annual reports: "Each year has seen some progress in annihilating distance and bringing people closer to each other. Thirty years more may bring about results which will be almost as astonishing as those of the past thirty years. To the public, this 'Bell System' furnishes facilities, in its 'universality' of service and connection . . . a service which could not be furnished by dissociated companies. The strength of the Bell System lies in this 'universality.'"

Vail's two main goals were to extend the long-distance network from coast to coast and interconnect all the telephones in between. The first depended on

The dial telephone was invented in 1889 by Almon Brown Strowger, a Kansas City undertaker, as a way to bypass Bell Company operators whom he suspected were referring customers to his competition. The dial telephone was available only to independent telephone company customers until the 1920s.

1878

1878

1880

1882

1886

1928

1949

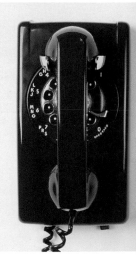

1956

During its history, the telephone has taken many shapes and forms, incorporating new advances in technology as well as changes in fashion: the early "butterstamp" telephone (1878), with the first handheld transmitter/ receiver; the hand-cranked wall set (1907); the first desk set (1928) that joined the separate transmitter and receiver into a single handheld instrument; the "500"-type desk set (1949), the common choice in America for decades; the Trimline Telephone (1968), which offered touch "dialing"; and the first cordless office phone (1989), which combined portability with a "hold" feature able to handle several calls at once.

1892

1896

1897

1907

1921

1964

1968

1989

Until 1992, the eighteen residents of Salmon Creek, Idaho, still used 1907 wall sets with hand cranks to signal an operator. Today, more than 94 percent of American households have phones, although about a third of the population of the world at large has still never made a single call.

The first public coin-operated pay phone was installed in the Hartford Bank in Hartford, Connecticut, in 1889. Until as late as the 1940s, many telephone companies issued tokens for use in their pay phones instead of coins.

67

Many of today's public telephones accept coins, pre-paid phone cards, or calling-card numbers, making it easy to call anywhere in the world.

These are some of the ways people answer the telephone in different countries around the world:

Argentina: Hola
Australia: Hello
Brazil: Alo
Canada: Hello
Denmark: (Say your name)
Egypt: Alo
Finland: (Say your name)
France: Allo
Germany: (Say your last name)
Great Britain: Hello
Greece: Geia sas
Hong Kong: Wei
Iceland: Hallo
Ireland: Hello
Israel: Shalom
Italy: Pronto
Japan: Moshi moshi
Kenya: Jambo
Korea: Yeo bo se yo
Mexico: Bueno
New Zealand: Hello
Norway: Hallo
Poland: Halo
Portugal: Alo
Russia: Allo
Saudi Arabia: Al salaam aleikum
Spain: Hola
Sweden: (Say your name)
Turkey: Efendim
Uganda: Jambo
United States: Hello

technological improvements, one of which had been made in 1900. Michael Pupin, a professor at Columbia University in New York, and George Campbell, a scientist employed by the Bell Company, had independently invented the loading coil, a device that processed the telephone signal at regular intervals along the line, and, by minimizing distortion, extended the range of a call. Using loading coils, the company was able to open a New York–Denver line in 1911. To get as far as California would take a new invention and another few years.

The second goal required a change of heart — and company policy — rather than technology. Like others at Bell, Vail was at first reluctant to give any ground to the independents. But he had come to see by late 1913 that a compromise was necessary. The company would allow the independents to use its long-distance lines in exchange for a share of the income. It would help end the confusion of competing local phone companies by selling its own companies or buying the others with government approval.

Vail's confidence in being close to reaching the last stage of his other goal — coast-to-coast connection — may have paved the way for compromise with the independents. Earlier that year, AT&T had purchased the rights to the final piece of technology that would make a transcontinental call possible: an amplifier, then called the vacuum-tube repeater, an electronic device that boosted signals as they traveled. Crews from San Francisco and Denver were already stringing lines to complete the cross-country network. They spliced them together on a telephone pole at the Utah–Nevada border on June 17, 1914. The total length of the historic line was over 4,300 miles.

On January 25, 1915, Alexander Graham Bell in New York City called Thomas Watson in San Francisco and repeated the historic words he had spoken thirty-nine years before, "Mr. Watson — Come here — I want to see you." This time Watson had to reply, "I should be very glad to, Dr. Bell, but we are now so far apart it would take me a week to come instead of a minute." The telephone had indeed gone a very long way.

Dial phones used automatic switchboards — instead of manual ones — to connect callers. One dial phone manufacturer promoted dial service as "secret service" (*opposite, top left*) since it connected calls without the need for a possibly eavesdropping operator. Direct dialing made the telephone the perfect communication medium for anyone needing privacy — from lovers (*opposite, bottom right: Oh Jeff ... I Love You Too, But*, by Roy Lichtenstein) to would-be military strategists (*opposite, bottom left:* Groucho Marx as Rufus T. Firefly, president of Fredonia, in *Duck Soup*, 1933).

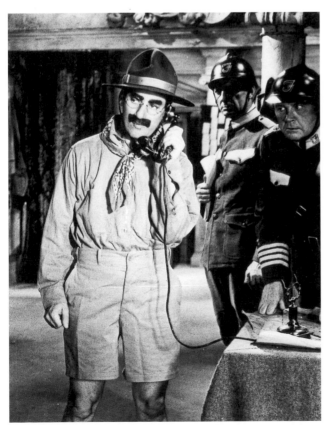

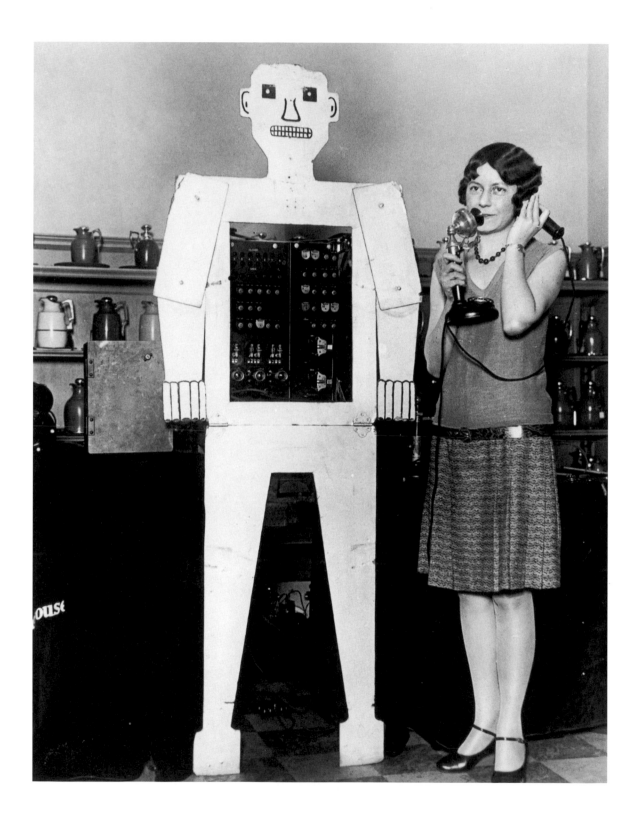

5

THE FUTURE OF LONG-
DISTANCE COMMUNICATION

From its earliest days, people have been predicting the future of the telephone. Some thought it wouldn't last because they couldn't see much need for it. "Of what use is such an invention?" asked an editor of the *New York World* in 1876. "Well, there may be occasions of state when it is necessary for officials who are far apart to talk with each other. Or some lover may wish to pop the question directly into the ear of a lady and hear for himself her reply, though miles away. It is not for us to guess how courtship will be carried on in the twentieth century."

Others were worried that the telephone would fall into the wrong hands and be a means for spreading dangerous ideas. One early prediction was that it would actually be used mostly for broadcasting news and entertainment — as the radio eventually would. Some saw its real potential — and more — right away, though it seemed fantastic at the time. Kate Field, an American journalist who helped Bell promote the phone in London in 1878, imagined the electronic age ahead (and remember, this was at a time when the lightbulb hadn't yet been invented): "Before long we shall sit down, fold our arms and let electricity do everything for us. We'll go to bed and get up by electricity. . . . We'll write by electricity and see by the same means. I've just read of the electro-

Opposite
Mr. Televox, one of the first "answering machines," designed by AT&T in the 1920s.

73

scope, the province of which is to transmit waves of light by electricity. Combine it with the Telephone, and while two persons, hundred of miles apart, are talking together, they will actually see each other!"

Bell's own prediction of the future of his invention was among the most accurate. Just after he had made the first telephone call to Watson on March 10, 1876, he wrote his father, "The day is coming when . . . wires will be laid on to houses just like water or gas — and friends will converse with each other without leaving home."

Before his death in 1922, Bell saw the groundwork laid for all this, and much, much more. Ever-growing demand coupled with ever-advancing technology took the phone farther and farther, faster and faster. The development of radio, which sent sound waves through the air, made possible "wireless" transmission, including the first two-way transatlantic call in 1926. Commercial overseas service began the next year, and in 1956 the first transatlantic telephone cable was laid — exactly a century after the telegraph had first made the same journey. In the late thirties and early forties, long-distance calls within the country were improved by a better insulated underground cable called coaxial, eventually able to carry over 100,000 conversations at once. And in 1962 came digital multiplexing, which changed the continuous undulating current into

a series of pulses (or bits) to represent the variations caused by the sound of the voice — a sort of late-twentieth-century version of Morse code that would eventually be used to carry text and images as well as sound. By the early seventies, the telephone could be found in 90 percent of American homes.

How will long-distance communication change in the years ahead? The future comes so quickly now that predictions seem to lag behind. But one thing is certain — the telephone is no longer just the telephone; it's part of a rapidly expanding telecommunications network that includes fax machines, the World Wide Web, E-mail, even cable television. The number of people using some combination of these services worldwide doubles every year.

When we say we're online today, we still mean we're on the telephone line, but we're as likely to be visiting a website or sending E-mail as we are to be talking on the phone. And the line we're on is less and less likely to be copper wire. Fiber optics now make it possible to send sound, text, and images by pulsing light — rather than by electricity — through hair-thin threads of glass or plastic. Bell himself had actually transmitted the voice by light waves using a "photophone" he invented in 1880. But it took another century before a strong enough light source (the laser) and transmitting material (glass fiber) made his idea practical. Now experts say that by the

Above left
In 1880, Bell made a working model of a "photophone" that transmitted speech on light waves. Not until the development of fiberoptic technology in the 1980s did this means of transmission become feasible over long distances.

Above right
The first full-color videophone that transmits both the image and the voice of the caller over regular telephone lines became available in 1992.

next century, we will be able to transmit the equivalent of all the world's television channels at one time over a single fiber-optic cable.

Eventually both wires and fiber-optic cables may disappear altogether, and transmission will be by radio waves through the air. Already it's common to see people talking on their cellular phones as they walk down the street or sit in restaurants. Bell Laboratories is working on a technology that will increase the speed and capacity of wireless transmission so that someday our home phones, cell phones, faxes, computers, pagers, and other devices will all be able to communicate with each other without any lines at all.

As the communications network gets faster and larger, the devices we connect to it get smarter and smaller. Already there are "intelligent" phones that can send and receive faxes and E-mail as well as regular calls (and of course the phone companies have kept pace with such services as call waiting, call forwarding, call conferencing, call answering, and caller I.D., which we take for granted). Soon there may be phones small enough to wear on our wrists that are activated by our voices rather than by pressing buttons. One research team has designed a pen with "digital ink" and a tiny built-in cell phone that would allow you to write a message on a napkin in your local coffee shop and E-mail it directly from there to your pen pal anywhere in the world. As computers get smaller too, there may be a time in the more distant future when phones, faxes, and computers — even video cameras and displays — converge into a single device that we'd wear, just like a belt or hat.

And as the different technologies converge, so do the businesses that supply them. As leading telecommunications companies merge in the late 1990s, it is as if they are once more trying to put Theodore Vail's vision of "one sys-

In the 1940s, Dick Tracy's two-way wrist radio (*above*) anticipated the voice-activated wrist cell phone demonstrated by an employee of the Japanese Nippon Telegraph and Telephone Corporation in 1996 (*opposite*).

tem" into practice — this time in a global sense — by being able to offer customers all the services of the network through a single provider.

At the end of the nineteenth century, we could converse with our distant friends without leaving home. At the end of the twentieth century, we can converse with them even if they aren't at home. We're so connected to each other now that you can call someone who lives a block away in New York City who's had her calls forwarded to her cell phone across the country so that you can talk to her while she's standing on a corner in Los Angeles. International corporations now regularly hold video conferences in which executives in one country "meet" with those in another without leaving their offices. Elementary school students in New Orleans can take a "field trip" to the rain forests of South America by a satellite videophone link while seated at their desks. Actors in a theater at Yale University in Connecticut can conduct interactive rehearsals over the Internet with actors in a theater in St. Petersburg, Russia.

What new possibilities does the next century hold? How will human beings communicate with each other over long distances in 2099? Will we be living on different planets and be able to send messages back and forth across light-years of space as we now can across continents? Will we still be carrying or wearing communication devices or will we somehow be able to beam our thoughts and words and images through the barriers of time and space by means we're currently unable to comprehend?

Even now, as you are reading this, billions of voice and data signals carrying the beginnings of the answers to some of these questions are circling the globe, branching out into the vast network of interconnected homes, offices, cars, street corners, rain forests, and mountain ranges that grew out of the attic workshop in Boston where the telephone was born just over a century ago.

FURTHER READING

Brooks, John. *Telephone: The First Hundred Years: The Wondrous Invention that Changed a World and Spawned a Corporate Giant.* New York: Harper & Row, 1975.

Bruce, Robert V. *Bell: Alexander Graham Bell and the Conquest of Solitude.* Boston: Little, Brown, 1973.

Eber, Dorothy Harley. *Genius at Work: Images of Alexander Graham Bell.* New York: Viking, 1982.

Fischer, Claude S. *America Calling: A Social History of the Telephone to 1940.* Berkeley: University of California Press, 1992.

Grosvenor, Edwin S. *Try It! The Alexander Graham Bell Science Kit Experiment Book.* Washington, D.C.: National Geographic Society, 1992.

Grosvenor, Edwin S. and Morgan Wesson. *Alexander Graham Bell: The Life and Times of the Man Who Invented the Telephone.* New York: Abrams, 1997.

Lampton, Christopher. *Telecommunications from Telegraphs to Modems.* New York: Franklin Watts, 1991.

Pasachoff, Naomi. *Alexander Graham Bell: Making Connections* (Oxford Portraits in Science). New York: Oxford University Press, 1996.

Skurzynski, Gloria. *Get the Message: Telecommunications in Your High Tech World.* New York: Bradbury Press, 1993.

St. George, Judith. *Dear Dr. Bell...Your Friend, Helen Keller.* New York: G. P. Putnam's Sons, 1992.

INDEX

Produced by
CommonPlace Publishing
2 Morse Court
New Canaan, Connecticut 06840

The text and display for this book have been typeset in various weights and sizes of Futura. A sans serif face designed in Germany in 1928 by Paul Renner, Futura has been widely copied and adapted for digital type systems. Based upon geometric shapes, the Futura letter is characterized by lines of uniform width. Previous typefaces reflected the irregularities of hand lettering.

We wish to express our gratitude to Morgan Wesson, Irene Lewicki at the AT&T Archives and Bunny White at Lucent Technologies Bell Labs Innovations whose advice and research enriched this book. The index was prepared by Elizabeth Miles Montgomery.

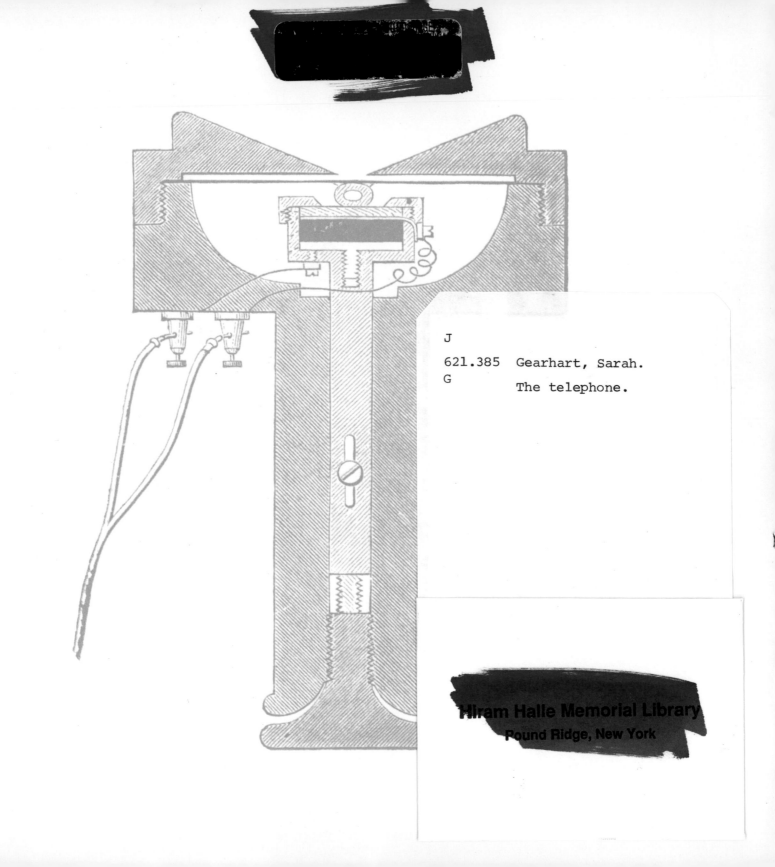